Contents

LADY LONG-LEGS

Nisba may be new at her school, but she's not going to let the older girls push her around!

Jan Mark is one of the most distinguished authors of books for young people. She has twice been awarded the Carnegie Medal and has also won the Penguin Guardian Award, the Observer Teenage Fiction Prize and the Angel Award for Fiction. Her many titles for Walker Books include *The Snow Maze* and *Taking the Cat's Way Home* as well as the picture books *Fur*, *Strat and Chatto* (Winner of the 1990 Mother Goose Award), *This Bowl of Earth*, *The Tale of Tobias* and *The Midas Touch*. Jan Mark lives in Oxford.

"An immensely satisfying story … demonstrates the very best in writing for developing readers."
The Sunday Telegraph

Books by the same author

The Snow Maze
Taking the Cat's Way Home

For older readers

The Eclipse of the Century
God's Story
The Lady with Iron Bones
Mr Dickens Hits Town
Nothing To Be Afraid Of
The Sighting
They Do Things Differently There
Thunder and Lightnings

Picture books

Fur
Strat and Chatto
The Tale of Tobias
The Midas Touch

JAN MARK

LADY LONG-LEGS

Illustrations by Paul Howard

WALKER BOOKS
AND SUBSIDIARIES

LONDON • BOSTON • SYDNEY

For Nisba, Neesa and Aishe

First published 1999 by
Walker Books Ltd, 87 Vauxhall Walk
London SE11 5HJ

This edition published 2001

2 4 6 8 10 9 7 5 3 1

Text © 1999 Jan Mark
Illustrations © 1999, 2001 Paul Howard

This book has been typeset in Garamond

Printed and bound in Great Britain
by The Guernsey Press Co. Ltd

British Library Cataloguing in Publication Data:
a catalogue record for this book is
available from the British Library

ISBN 0-7445-8296-2

Chapter One

Nisba was a new girl. Everyone else in her class had been at Farm Lane School for three years and one term. Nisba had been there for three days.

It was cold and frosty outside, but the hall was warm and cosy.

After assembly, Nisba said to Mr Martin, "Where does the warm come from?"

"Warmth," Mr Martin said. "Do you know what, Nisba? You are the first person who has ever asked me that."

Mr Martin liked people to ask him questions. He was not so happy when they told him things. They told him things all day long.

"Sir, Neesa's got mud on her shoes."

"Mr Martin, Aishe's taken my crayons."

"Farid's hitting Robert, Sir."

Nisba was new. She had nothing to tell him yet.

"We have under-floor heating," Mr Martin said. "There are hot pipes down there under the floor tiles. That is why the tiles keep coming unstuck. The glue melts and the tiles split."

The floor of the hall was red and black tiles, but in places there were blue tiles instead of black ones, and pink tiles instead of red ones. Mr Keates, the caretaker, never had enough of the right colours when he mended the floor.

And there was one white tile, almost in the middle of the doorway. Nisba had learned one important thing already. It was very bad luck to walk on the white tile.

If someone walked on the white  tile they had to stand on one leg and count to twenty, with their fingers crossed. Otherwise they got bad luck.

On the very first day Robert had fallen down the steps in the corridor and broken his arm. Everyone said it was because he walked on the white tile going in to assembly and didn't bother to count to twenty with his fingers crossed.

Robert said it was because Farid had pushed him, but everyone knew about the white tile. Aishe had seen him walk on it.

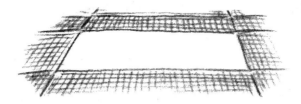

Chapter Two

Nisba was not afraid of the white tile in the hall, so she walked on it. People said that if you stood on a blue tile and a pink tile at the same time, all your teeth would fall out. No one dared to try it.

Mr Keates did it all the time. He had false teeth.

It was different in the corridor. In the corridor the tiles were brown.

"Brown is the colour of footprints," Mr Martin said. "The colour of mud and dust and old, old dinner."

But not all of the tiles were brown. Down the middle of the corridor there was a pattern like a hopscotch grid, made of green and yellow tiles.

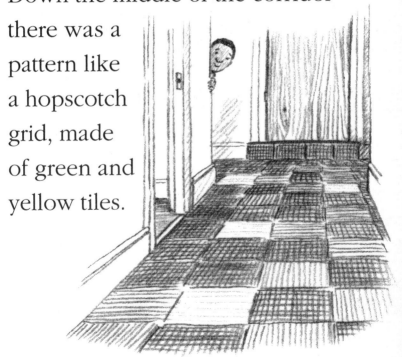

They were not allowed to play hopscotch indoors but the patterns were not wasted. Some people would walk only on brown tiles.

Some people took big steps and walked only on yellow tiles. The ones with very long legs could get all the way from the front door to the hall on green tiles.

The six steps by the staff room were all brown. They did not count.

Nisba had long legs. On the fourth day of term she went right down the corridor on green tiles, but as she passed the cloakroom a big girl came out. It was Lucy Wells.

"You can't do that," Lucy said. "It's not allowed."

"What isn't?" Nisba said.

"Only people in Year 4 can walk on green tiles," Lucy said.

Nisba looked at Lucy. "What year are you in?"

"Year 4," Lucy said. "You're not in Year 4."

Nisba took a big step from one green tile to the next.

Lucy stamped. "You can't do that!"

"Yes I can," Nisba said, and took another step.

Lucy gave her a hard push.

"If I see you walking on green tiles again, you'll be in trouble."

Mrs Higgins came along. She was the Head Teacher.

"You ought to be in your classrooms now," she said. "Hurry up."

Lucy went into the Year 4 room. As she opened the door she turned round and gave Nisba a nasty look.

"Stay off those green tiles," Lucy said. "Daddy-long-legs."

Chapter Three

"I've got another question," Nisba
said to Mr Martin. "Why can't Year 3
people walk on the green tiles?"

"I don't know," Mr Martin said.
"Tell me about it."

Nisba did not want to tell tales.

"In the corridor," she said, "there are lots of brown tiles and some yellow tiles and not many green tiles. Someone said only Year 4 people can walk on the green tiles."

"Ah, I see," said Mr Martin. "Well, once upon a time, people used to play hopscotch on the yellow and green tiles, and there were accidents, so the rule is, no jumping. But Year 4 people are taller. They can take bigger steps. There's no rule about that."

"I can take bigger steps too," Nisba said.

Mr Martin looked at her.

"You're a very tall girl, Nisba," he said. "You go ahead and walk where you like."

At lunch-time, Nisba went up the corridor on the green tiles, and into the cloakroom.

Lucy Wells was waiting for her.

"I saw you walking on the green tiles," Lucy said. She had friends with her.

"Mr Martin said I could walk on them," Nisba said. "Mr Martin says I can walk where I like."

"It's nothing to do with him," said one of Lucy's friends. "We say you can't."

"Anyway," Lucy said, "you're a new girl. New girls can only walk on brown tiles. Everyone knows that."

Nisba looked at Lucy and Lucy's friends. None of them was as tall as Nisba. Suddenly she understood. They were angry because she *could* reach the green tiles without jumping, not because she *did*.

Silly little things, Nisba thought. She went out of the cloakroom and stood on a green tile. Someone behind her hooked a foot round her ankle. She lost her balance and fell over, hitting her arm on the step at the bottom of the staircase.

Chapter Four

Mrs Higgins came out of the staff room and saw Nisba sitting on the floor. Nisba was trying not to cry. Lucy was pretending that she had just come out of the cloakroom. Lucy's friends began to look at a picture on the wall.

"Lucy and Nisba *again?*" Mrs Higgins said. "I hope you're not fighting."

"I slipped on the tiles," Nisba said.

"Yes, she slipped," said Lucy, and Lucy's friends.

Nisba stood up. She had a big red mark on her arm.

"That will be a nasty bruise," Mrs Higgins said. "You need the Hand of Peace on that. Go to the staff room and say I sent you. The rest of you get your lunch."

Nisba went up the steps to the staff room and knocked on the door.

Miss Shah came out. "Who are you?" she said.

"I'm Nisba," Nisba said. "I'm new. Mrs Higgins says I need the Hand of Peace."

She showed Miss Shah her bruise.

"Come in, then," Miss Shah said. "How did you do that?"

"I slipped and fell on the steps," Nisba said. She followed Miss Shah into the staff room.

All the teachers were sitting in comfy chairs, eating their lunch and drinking coffee. In the corner was a sink, and a draining board, and a little fridge.

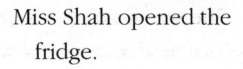

Miss Shah opened the fridge.

"Will it hurt?" Nisba said, as Miss Shah took something out of the ice box.

"You tell me," Miss Shah said. "It looks as if it hurts already."

"No, not my arm. The Hand of Peace."

Miss Shah laughed. "It's not the Hand of *Peace*, Nisba, it's the Hand of *Peas*. Someone found out that a good thing for a bruise is to put a packet of frozen peas on it. We've got something even better."

She was holding a white plastic glove, tied at the wrist with string.

"The peas are in the glove," Miss Shah said. "Go and sit in the front hall for a bit. Hold the glove against your poor arm and it will feel like a nice cool hand."

Chapter Five

The front hall was a good place to sit. There were armchairs for visitors, and a piece of carpet, and three tall plants in pots.

Nisba had sat here once before, with Mum, when they came to ask Mrs Higgins if Nisba could go to Farm Lane School.

Nisba took the best chair and held
the Hand of Peas against her bruise.
It was so cold she could feel it
making the swelling go down. It felt
like peace, even if it was only
frozen peas.

From her chair Nisba could see past the staff room, down the steps and along the corridor.

Mrs Higgins was there, with Mr Keates the caretaker. They were crawling about, poking the floor.

Mrs Higgins did not often crawl about on the floor. She had nice trousers on, too.

"Here's another," Mr Keates said. "Split right across. It's those pipes again."

"One of the little ones tripped just now," Mrs Higgins said.

That's me, Nisba thought. They think I tripped on a loose tile. But I'm not little. That's the trouble.

Mrs Higgins came back up the steps and saw Nisba.

"Better now?" she said.

"Yes, thank you," Nisba said.

"Go and have your lunch, then," Mrs Higgins said. She went into her special room with HEAD TEACHER on the door.

Nisba took the Hand of Peas off her arm. Now her skin was icy cold and the Hand was warm and floppy. She knocked on the door of the staff room. Miss Shah came to take the Hand away.

"I'll put it back in the fridge to get cold for someone else," she said.

Nisba walked down the steps and along the corridor. Now that she was looking for them she could see the split tiles. Some of the green tiles were split, but she stepped on them anyway, because Lucy had said she must not.

She did not really want to walk on green tiles all the time, but Lucy was a bully, and bullies must never be allowed to win.

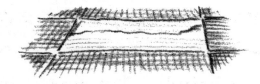

Chapter Six

Then it was Saturday. There was no
school for two whole days, so Nisba
wore her bangles. But every time
she looked at her arm she saw the
fading bruise, and thought of Lucy.

Was Lucy a bully? Bullies were supposed to be big and tough. Nisba was bigger than Lucy, but Lucy had friends.

Four little bullies were as bad as one big one.

On Monday it was very cold. As Nisba walked across the playground she thought of the warm floor in the hall where they would sit for assembly.

She hung up her coat in the cloakroom and went into the corridor. Something had happened. Something was different.

It was the floor.

During the weekend Mr Keates had been at work. Nisba remembered how he had crawled on the floor with Mrs Higgins, counting split tiles. He had taken them all away and put new ones down.

The new tiles were grey, and they were all over the place. Some of them were in the hopscotch patterns instead of green tiles or yellow ones. No one could walk down the corridor on only green tiles now, they were too far apart.

Not even Mr Martin would be able to do it, and he was the tallest teacher.

At the end of the corridor by the Year 4 room, people were trying to walk on green tiles. Lucy took a huge step but it was no use, she could not reach.

"Nyah, nyah," Lucy said, when she saw Nisba. "Now you'll have to walk on the brown tiles, Daddy-long-legs."

"No I won't," Nisba said, and she walked all the way down the corridor on the new grey tiles. It was the hardest thing she had ever done and she nearly fell over twice, but she stepped on every grey tile.

Lucy and her friends were growling.

When Nisba got to the end of the corridor they all started to walk the other way, but no one else could step on all the grey tiles. They had to hop between some of them.

Neesa and Aishe were watching. They went into the Year 3 room and fetched Mr Martin. They knew what Lucy was like. They knew what Lucy had done to Nisba.

"People are jumping in the corridor," Neesa said. "They mustn't do that, must they?"

"No," said Mr Martin, and he came out to see what was going on.

Chapter Seven

"Here comes Mr Martin. Look out!"
said one of Lucy's friends.

Lucy was just starting to jump. She
tried to stop but it was too late, and
she sat down hard on the floor.

"What's all this?" Mr Martin said.
Lucy started to cry.

"Have you hurt yourself?" Mr
Martin said.

"I bumped my head," Lucy said.
It was not true. She had bumped
her bottom but she did not want to
say so.

"Go and get the Hand of Peas,"
Mr Martin said. "If we have any more
accidents they will close the school.
Now, what are you all doing?"

No one said anything.

"I hear you have been jumping,"
Mr Martin said. "Were you playing
hopscotch? You know that is not
allowed."

"I was walking on the grey tiles," Nisba said. "I wasn't jumping."

Lucy came back. She had the Hand of Peas on her head. "I didn't jump," she said. "Not really, I didn't. I just didn't quite walk."

"And I can't quite fly," Mr Martin said. "Jumping is both feet off the ground at once. I know all about how you walk on special tiles, but walking is not jumping. Let's see who can do it. Start at the steps and see how far you get."

One after the other the Year 4 people tried to walk down the corridor, stepping only on the new grey tiles, but no one could do it.

"Now Nisba," Mr Martin said, and Nisba went down the corridor again, stepping on the grey tiles.

"That's not fair," Lucy said. "She's only got a little bit of her foot on some of those tiles."

"It is fair," Aishe said. "Robert only had a tiny bit of his foot on the white tile, but he still broke his arm."

"This could get dangerous," Mr Martin said. "What have you started, Nisba?"

"I'm sorry," Nisba said, but she did not think she had done anything wrong.

"You need not be sorry," Mr Martin said, "but are you always going to walk on the grey tiles?"

"No," Nisba said. "It hurts my legs where they join on. I just wanted to see if I could."

"There," Mr Martin said. "Do you understand? You don't *have* to do something just because you *can*. If Nisba stops walking on the grey tiles, will the rest of you stop trying to?"

They all nodded, but Lucy hissed, "Daddy-long-legs."

"Stop it, Lucy," Mr Martin said. "And do put that horrible Hand back in the fridge. It looks as if someone is trying to pull your head off."

"Nisba can't be a daddy," Neesa
said. "She's a girl."

"She'll be a lady, not a daddy,"
Aishe said.

And Nisba said, "That's right. I'm
Lady Long-legs."

More Sprinters for you to enjoy!

- *Little Stupendo Flies High* Jon Blake   0-7445-5970-7

- *Captain Abdul's Pirate School* Colin McNaughton 0-7445-5242-7

- *The Ghost in Annie's Room* Philippa Pearce   0-7445-5993-6

- *Molly and the Beanstalk* Pippa Goodhart   0-7445-5981-2

- *Taking the Cat's Way Home* Jan Mark   0-7445-8268-7

- *The Finger-eater* Dick King-Smith   0-7445-8269-5

- *Care of Henry* Anne Fine   0-7445-8270-9

- *The Impossible Parents Go Green* Brian Patten   0-7445-7881-7

- *Flora's Fantastic Revenge* Nick Warburton   0-7445-7898-1

- *Jolly Roger* Colin McNaughton   0-7445-8293-8

- *The Haunting of Pip Parker* Anne Fine   0-7445-8294-6

- *Tarquin the Wonder Horse* June Crebbin   0-7445-7882-5

- *Cup Final Kid* Martin Waddell   0-7445-8297-0

- *Lady Long-legs* Jan Mark   0-7445-8296-2

- *Ronnie and the Giant Millipede* Jenny Nimmo   0-7445-8298-9

All at £3.99